Logansport Cass County Public Library

J F SUT

Sutherland, Margaret.

Thanks____ ___ s for giving

D1237458

WITHDRAWN

Thanksgiving is for Giving Thanks

By Margaret Sutherland
Illustrated by Sonja Lamut

To Owen, for whom I give the ultimate thanks—Margaret

To my daughter, Anna—Sonja

Grosset & Dunlap, Publishers

Copyright © 2000 by Grosset & Dunlap. Illustrations copyright © 2000 by Sonja Lamut. All rights reserved. Published by Grosset & Dunlap, a division of Penguin Putnam Books for Young Readers, New York. GROSSET & DUNLAP is a trademark of Penguin Putnam Inc. Published simultaneously in Canada. Printed in the U.S.A.

Library of Congress Cataloging-in-Publication Data

Sutherland, Margaret.
Thanksgiving is for giving thanks / by Margaret Sutherland ; illustrated by Sonja Lamut.
p. cm — (Reading railroad books)
Summary: A child lists all the things for which he is thankful, especially at Thanksgiving.
[1. Gratitude—Fiction. 2. Thanksgiving Day—Fiction.] I. Lamut, Sonja, ill. II. Title. III. Series.
PZ7.S9668 Th 2000 [E]—dc21 00-055137

ISBN 0-448-42286-7   G H I J

Thanksgiving is the day of the year that we eat lots of turkey and pumpkin pie.

But most of all, it is the day when we give thanks
for all the things that make us feel happy.

I am thankful for my dad and mom.
They love me when I'm good...

...and even when I'm not so good.

I am thankful for everyone else in my family.

My grandma gives really good hugs.

I am thankful for my teacher.

She makes me feel special when she hangs
my artwork on the wall.

I am thankful for my friends,
who make me laugh.

I am thankful for my room.

Sometimes it's nice to be by myself.

I am thankful for hot chocolate
on a cold, rainy day.

I am thankful for all the dogs
and cats that I know.

It's fun when they let me pet them.

I am thankful for my favorite books. I like bedtime when Mom or Dad reads to me.

I am thankful for bright sunny days when I can play outside with my friends.

I am thankful for lollipops
that turn my tongue purple...

...or green or orange
or red or blue.

I am thankful for special days like Thanksgiving, when I'm with my whole family and we can all be thankful together.